EASTLAKE PUBLIC LIBRARY
36706 LAKE SHORE BLVD.
EASTLAKE, OHIO 44095

Gary Payton

Additional Titles in the Sports Reports Series

Andre Agassi
Star Tennis Player
(0-89490-798-0)

Troy Aikman
Star Quarterback
(0-89490-927-4)

Roberto Alomar
Star Second Baseman
(0-7660-1079-1)

Charles Barkley
Star Forward
(0-89490-655-0)

Terrell Davis
Star Running Back
(07660-1331-6)

Tim Duncan
Star Forward
(0-7660-1334-0)

Dale Earnhardt
Star Race Car Driver
(0-7660-1335-9)

Brett Favre
Star Quarter Back
(0-7660-1332-4)

Jeff Gordon
Star Race Car Driver
(0-7660-1083-X)

Wayne Gretzky
Star Center
(0-89490-930-4)

Ken Griffey, Jr.
Star Outfielder
(0-89490-802-2)

Scott Hamilton
Star Figure Skater
(0-7660-1236-0)

Anfernee Hardaway
Star Guard
(0-7660-1234-4)

Grant Hill
Star Forward
(0-7660-1078-3)

Michael Jordan
Star Guard
(0-89490-482-5)

Shawn Kemp
Star Forward
(0-89490-929-0)

Jason Kidd
Star Guard
(0-7660-1333-2)

Mario Lemieux
Star Center
(0-89490-932-0)

Karl Malone
Star Forward
(0-89490-931-2)

Dan Marino
Star Quarterback
(0-89490-933-9)

Mark McGwire
Star Home Run Hitter
(0-7660-1329-4)

Mark Messier
Star Center
(0-89490-801-4)

Reggie Miller
Star Guard
(0-7660-1082-1)

Chris Mullin
Star Forward
(0-89490-486-8)

Hakeem Olajuwon
Star Center
(0-89490-803-0)

Shaquille O'Neal
Star Center
(0-89490-656-9)

Scottie Pippen
Star Forward
(0-7660-1080-5)

Jerry Rice
Star Wide Receiver
(0-89490-928-2)

Cal Ripken, Jr.
Star Shortstop
(0-89490-485-X)

David Robinson
Star Center
(0-89490-483-3)

Barry Sanders
Star Running Back
(0-89490-484-1)

Deion Sanders
Star Athlete
(0-89490-652-6)

Junior Seau
Star Linebacker
(0-89490-800-6)

Emmitt Smith
Star Running Back
(0-89490-653-4)

Frank Thomas
Star First Baseman
(0-89490-659-3)

Thurman Thomas
Star Running Back
(0-89490-445-0)

Chris Webber
Star Forward
(0-89490-799-9)

Tiger Woods
Star Golfer
(0-7660-1081-3)

Steve Young
Star Quarterback
(0-89490-654-2)

SPORTS REPORTS

Gary Payton

Star Guard

Ross Bernstein

Willoughby-Eastlake
Public Library

Enslow Publishers, Inc.
40 Industrial Road   PO Box 38
Box 398   Aldershot
Berkeley Heights, NJ 07922   Hants GU12 6BP
USA   UK
http://www.enslow.com

Copyright © 2000 by Ross Bernstein

All rights reserved.

No part of this book may be reproduced by any means without the written permission of the publisher.

Library of Congress Cataloging-in-Publication Data

Bernstein, Ross.
    Gary Payton, star guard / Ross Bernstein.
       p. cm. — (Sports reports)
    Includes bibliographical references (p.) and index.
    Summary: Profiles the personal life and professional career of the guard for the Seattle SuperSonics, Gary Payton.
    ISBN 0-7660-1330-8
    1. Payton, Gary, 1968– Juvenile literature. 2. Basketball players—United States Biography Juvenile literature. [1. Payton, Gary, 1968– . 2. Basketball players. 3. Afro-Americans Biography.]
    I. Title II. Series.
GV884.A39B47   2000
796.323'092—dc21
[B]   99-31675
                                                                                                  CIP

Printed in the United States of America.

10 9 8 7 6 5 4 3 2 1

To Our Readers: All Internet addresses in this book were active and appropriate when we went to press. Any comments or suggestions can be sent by e-mail to Comments@enslow.com or to the address on the back cover.

Photo Credits: Bill Alkofer, St. Paul Pioneer Press, pp. 45, 52, 54, 60, 63, 65, 71, 74, 78, 84, 87, 91; Dave Nishitani, Oregon State University Athletic Department, pp. 27, 37; Fred Noel, Skyline High School, p. 23; Oregon State University Athletic Department, pp. 11, 15, 34, 40; Steve Shields, Oregon State University Athletic Department, p. 49.

Cover Photo: Sam Forencich/NBA Photos

Contents

1 Going for the Gold 7

2 Hoop Dreams From Oakland 19

3 How OSU Became
"Payton's Place" 31

4 "The Glove" Takes Seattle
by Storm 43

5 Losing Two Heartbreakers 57

6 Running With the Bulls 69

7 The Future Is Bright 81

Chapter Notes 96

Career Statistics 100

Where to Write 101

Index 103

Chapter 1

Going for the Gold

After leading the Seattle SuperSonics to the National Basketball Association (NBA) Championship series in 1996 only to lose a heartbreaker to the mighty Chicago Bulls, one would think that Gary Payton might want to take the summer off to relax. After all, wouldn't the league's Defensive Player of the Year want a little rest after playing a grueling eighty-two-game schedule? Nope. Not Gary Payton. He was going to go for the gold, as in medal, that is. You see, he had been selected to become a member of the now infamous "Dream Team III," which contained twelve of the NBA's best players. Gary Payton would be representing the United States in the 1996 Olympic Games in Atlanta,

Georgia. "I was honored to get the call," said Payton. "It's a great experience for me to wear the USA on my chest and get a chance for the gold. It's a great opportunity."[1]

The opportunity for Payton to finally win a gold medal in international basketball competition was a dream come true for the All-Star point guard. He had come up short on previous attempts, and he knew that this might be his last chance for gold. Twice before, he had earned silver medals as a member of the 1987 USA Basketball Junior World Championship team and the 1989 USA Basketball World Championship qualifying team. In 1988 he participated in the Olympic team trials, but he failed to make the team's final cut. Payton regretted not being selected to that gold-medal-winning squad and wanted to win now more than ever.

As a member of Dream Team III, Payton would be called on to do the two things that he loved to do best: "dish" and "dis." This meant dishing out assists to his teammates and also stopping opposing ball handlers on defense. For Payton, it was a wonderful experience to be included with the world's best players. "Being with these guys is great," said Payton of his new teammates. "You get to see what Charles Barkley is like off the court, which is an adventure. Me and John Stockton, we go after each other [during the NBA season]. It's good for me to see what he's like off the court."[2]

With the combination of veteran players combined with incredibly talented young superstars, how could head coach Lenny Wilkens possibly choose who would play? The coach decided that he was going to change his starting lineup for every game. However, there were two players who would always play. "All I know for sure is that I want Scottie Pippen and Gary Payton in the game," Wilkens said. "After that, it doesn't really matter."[3] In an interview, Wilkens talked more about his game philosophy:

> There is no question that when you put together a team like that, everyone expects you to win. And we're playing at home, too. It will be a lot of pressure. But my motto is to be prepared and we'll be prepared. The thing I have to do is tell the players to play the game as well as they can and show the world how good we really are. I want them to show the world that basketball is still really our game.[4]

The expectations were high for the team. It was competing as much against rival teams as it was against the memory of the original Dream Team, which starred Michael Jordan, Magic Johnson, and Larry Bird, among others. That squad went on to earn a gold medal in the 1992 Olympics in

Barcelona, Spain, winning by an average margin of forty-four points per game. Dream Team II also brought home the gold at the 1994 World Championships in Toronto, Canada. Now, with the eyes of the nation watching, Gary Payton and Dream Team III set out to establish their own identity.

After playing a brief exhibition schedule, the Dream Teamers kicked off the centennial Olympiad in Atlanta's Georgia Dome. The first game was against the Argentine national team. The Americans were plagued by early turnovers and got off to a slow start. Then, with Argentina leading, 15–14, something happened that swung the momentum back in favor of the Americans. With twelve and a half minutes to go in the first half, a power failure knocked some of the lights out in the arena. After a ten-minute delay, the lights came back on, and David Robinson's three-point shot gave the United States the lead for good. The Dream Team had piled up an eleven-point lead before the Argentines whittled it back down to just two at the half, 46–44. The Americans came out and played inspired basketball in the second half and rallied in the final quarter for a 96–68 win. The game was brought to a thunderous end when Payton threw a long breakaway pass to his new pal from the Los Angeles Lakers, Shaquille

Being selected as a member of the Dream Team meant that Gary Payton would be recognized as one of the world's elite basketball players.

O'Neal, whose monster slam dunk brought the fans to their feet.

Next up for the Dream Team was Angola, but without anyone taller than six feet six inches on the Angolan team, the game got ugly early on. Payton picked apart the Angolan defense, forcing its members to shoot low-percentage shots mostly from the perimeter. He led the Americans to a convincing 87–54 triumph, improving their record to 2–0.

In the third game, the Dream Team knew it was going to have to play better. Starting slowly, and then using its superior size and strength, Team USA wore down a respectable Lithuanian team that hung tough. Led by Payton's 8 points and 4 assists, the Americans pulled away in the second half for a 104–82 victory. Payton, who was really enjoying the celebrity spotlight that was shining brightly on him and his squad, was featured in many national television interviews as a spokesperson for the team.

In the fourth game of the tournament, which was against China, Payton showed the world why his up-close, aggressive defensive skills had earned him the nickname "the Glove." (He covers opposing players like a glove covers a hand.) In addition to his 9 assists, he also guided a defense that created 21 steals and forced 33 turnovers. The United States team crushed the Chinese by a score of 133–70,

FACT

The 1996 Dream Team Roster included Orlando center Shaquille O'Neal, Houston center Hakeem Olajuwon, San Antonio center David Robinson, Chicago forward Scottie Pippen, Utah forward Karl Malone, Detroit forward Grant Hill, Phoenix forward Charles Barkley, Orlando guard Anfernee "Penny" Hardaway, Indiana guard Reggie Miller, Utah guard John Stockton, and Sacramento guard Mitch Richmond.

while playing in front of a record Olympic basketball crowd of 34,417 spectators at the Georgia Dome. Payton, who at times seemingly toyed with the Chinese players with his unbelievable fakeouts and lightning-quick passes, did not even attempt a shot during the game. When asked why after the game, he calmly replied with a smile: "Didn't have to!"[5]

The Dream Teamers continued to roll, next beating Croatia, 102–71. It was a rough game that pitted two NBA teammates against each other: Scottie Pippen and Tony Kukoc, both members of the Chicago Bulls. After jumping out to a 12–0 run to open the game, the defense took over. The Americans, whose pressure defense forced 15 steals, were once again led by Gary Payton who scored 7 points, 7 assists, and 4 rebounds.

Later that week, Team USA faced a very skilled Brazil club. Payton would be called on to guard an international legend, Oscar Schmidt, the leading scorer in Olympic basketball history. Payton hung tough against the Brazilian sharpshooter, and neutralized him to only seven points in the second half. Payton also put on a razzle-dazzle display midway through the second half when he fed Shaquille O'Neal on two alley-oop dunks. Payton finished with 7 points, 7 assists, and 5 rebounds, as the

Dream Team advanced to the semifinals with a 98–45 win over Brazil.

In the semifinals, the Americans faced a tough Australian team that featured several current and former NBA players. Charles Barkley took over the scrappy, physical game. He scored 24 points and added 11 rebounds in a 101–73 victory. Payton added 6 points, 4 rebounds, and 2 assists, as Team USA pulled away in the second half. For Payton, who desperately wanted to put a gold medal around his neck instead of a silver one, it would all come down to one more game against the Yugoslav national team.

Yugoslavia, which came into the game with an identical 7–0 Olympic record, was not to be overlooked. It had two NBA players in its starting lineup: Vlade Divac of the Charlotte Hornets and Sasha Danilovic of the Miami Heat.

As the game got under way, the Dream Team's starting lineup of Gary Payton, Scottie Pippen, Karl Malone, Reggie Miller, and Hakeem Olajuwon missed its first six shots. Yugoslavia, on the other hand, came out strong and outscored the United States for the first sixteen minutes of the contest. The Americans trailed by as many as seven points and did not take their first lead of the game, 36–35, until three minutes and fourteen seconds remained

Payton is known as "the Glove" because he covers opposing players like a glove covers a hand.

before the intermission. Payton was playing outstanding defense, and he was thrilling the record crowd of more than thirty-four thousand fans at the Georgia Dome by feeding spectacular blind passes to his teammates.

At halftime, the Yugoslavs trailed by only five points. Team USA needed a jump start, and it got one. In a stirring ceremony at the half, boxer Muhammad Ali received a ceremonial gold medal. The medal honored his championship performance at the 1960 Olympic Games in Rome. For Payton, who had idolized Ali since he was a child, the ceremony inspired him to play even harder in the second half.

Yugoslavia would not give up, though. With only fourteen minutes left in the game, the Yugoslavs found themselves down only 51–50. Payton hollered at his teammates to stay focused and hang tough. In this group of the world's elite basketball players, Payton stood out as their emotional leader. He was the defensive catalyst and assist-maker for the team, and he knew how to get his teammates fired up to win. Payton was closer to gold than he had ever been and knew that he had to stay focused.

The Americans came out and dominated the game from that point on. John Stockton saved a ball that was going out of bounds with 6:26 to play. In one motion, he threw the ball over his head, down the length of the court, and to his teammate Reggie Miller for a monster jam. The United States went on to win the game, 95–69. For Payton, who had just turned twenty-eight earlier that week, this was one "golden birthday" that he was surely going to remember for a lifetime.

Chapter 2

Hoop Dreams From Oakland

Gary Dwayne Payton was born on July 23, 1968, in East Oakland, California. He grew up in a family that loved sports. His parents, Al and Annie Payton, had five children: Greg, Alfred, Sharon, Winnie, and Gary. They encouraged and supported athletics as an important part of their children's education. Gary, the youngest of the bunch, enjoyed many activities, including football, baseball, biking, and tennis, but it was basketball that became his true love. It was also basketball that kept him out of trouble.

A kid could grow up pretty fast on the streets of East Oakland. Drugs, crime, and poverty were nearby. And for many kids, growing up in that type of environment meant trouble. However, Gary had one thing going for him that many kids did not—a strict and loving father who not only had an incredible love for the game of basketball but also made sure that his son stayed out of trouble.

Al Payton was a dedicated family man. He worked several restaurant jobs, as well as at a cannery, so that his children could have the things that he did not have as a child. Al, himself a former basketball guard at Alcorn A&M University, coached in the Oakland Neighborhood Basketball League. He worked on the fine art of defense with Gary, and if the father felt that the son was not performing up to his standards, he would let the boy sit on the bench for a while to think about what he needed to do to be a better ballplayer.

Ever the competitor, Al Payton pushed little Gary to be not only a good basketball player but also tough. Al insisted that if Gary was going to talk the talk, he had better be able to walk the walk. Things often got heated on the playground, but Gary could hold his own. "We would say anything [in a game]," recalled Gary. "Just a lot of yappity-yap talk."[1]

On the playgrounds of East Oakland, basketball was like religion—and Big Al was the preacher. "Discipline. That's why he is so good. I had him on a very tight schedule," said Al. "I made him take vitamins, eat his vegetables, and kept him off the streets."²

Gary Payton stood out from the other kids. People could tell early on that he had a lot of raw talent. It was at Jefferson Elementary School that Gary became a playground legend. "Jefferson is where I learned the game, where I learned to play my tough defense—I had no other choice," Payton later recalled.³

After junior high, Gary wanted to attend Fremont High School. It was close to home, and most of his friends were going to go there. But Gary's father insisted that his son attend Skyline High School, which was located in a mostly white neighborhood. Gary resisted, but then, just before the enrollment deadline, there was a fatal stabbing during a fight on the playground at Fremont. Skyline now sounded like a great choice.

His new school came with new friends, new teammates, and plenty of distractions. So many distractions, in fact, that Gary's grades really suffered. During his sophomore year, his casual attitude toward studying got him suspended from the basketball team for nearly half the season. "I messed up—fighting, trashing teachers and coaches, everybody," said Payton.⁴ Of course, that did not sit well with his dad. "He was running at the mouth

FACT

Growing up, Payton's favorite player was George Gervin. Known as "the Ice Man," Gervin was one of the NBA's original slam dunkers. The former San Antonio Spur could glide through the air for what seemed like an eternity and then drop the ball into the net with his patented "finger roll."

with his teachers and things," recalled Al Payton."[5] As a result, Al instituted his "tough love" program. For a couple of days a week, and for nearly two months, Al Payton went to school with Gary. One time, Al even came barging into Gary's classroom to reprimand his son, humiliating him in front of his classmates. "I started growing up," said Payton.[6]

"He [Gary] came in as a sophomore at around 5-foot-6, and he thought that all he had to do was put his feet on the court to be a starter on my team," said Skyline basketball coach Fred Noel. "At first, he just wanted to play ball and didn't really care about that 'academic stuff.' So, he sat out most of his first season because of poor grades."[7] Gary then began to think about attending college after high school. Knowing that the college entrance exams were getting tougher and tougher, Gary settled down, worked harder at his studies, and focused on basketball. At the time, Skyline was not considered to be a basketball powerhouse by any means. It played in the Oakland Athletic League, arguably one of the toughest in California, maybe in the country. In Gary's sophomore season, his team went 1–9 in league play. That next summer, Coach Noel wanted his players to start building some chemistry together as a team. He had them lifting weights, training hard, and hanging out together. In addition, they also played a tough 60-game summer schedule.

The Oakland Athletic League games were fiercely competitive. Because there was an occasional outburst of violence at many of the games, the contests were held during the afternoons. Gary's dad and older brother Alfred (who played basketball at San Francisco State) escorted Gary to and from his games.

This environment would scare most kids away, make them timid, or even force them to quit, but not Gary. He loved it and even thrived in it, all because

Gary Payton (back row, third from the right) and Coach Noel (back row, far right) are still good friends today.

he had the gift of gab. Even though Gary was small, he knew that he could hold his own on the court against his opponents. He had learned that unless you got in your opponent's face, you would be considered a wimp. If his opponents considered him a wimp, they would not respect him.

"Gary has always been a talker, that's just part of the way that he learned how to play the game," said Coach Noel. "He even learned how to talk to an opponent without his lips even moving, because he knew that if I saw him trash-talking, that I would sit him down."[8] But as Payton explained, "You talk about rowdy, in Oakland the players were on you. The refs were on you. The stands were on you. You had to talk back or you were a sissy; you'd get run out of the league."[9]

Skyline had not won a league title for more than twenty-five years, and it was eager to show the Bay Area that it had arrived. Gary soon began to emerge as a star in the league. Even though he was small, he was lightning quick and loved to pass the ball. One of the other stars of the team was the six-foot-eleven center named Greg Foster. Having Greg on the team gave Gary a lot of options and helped him develop his passing skills. Gary Payton was becoming very confident in his abilities to pass, shoot, steal, and defend.

As a junior, Gary garnered second-team, All-East Bay honors. That season he averaged 18.3 points, 10.3 assists, and 4.1 rebounds per game, leading Skyline to a 19–7 record and a league title. The team advanced to the Northern California Championship; they eventually lost to Logan High School on a last-second shot. The Skyline High School Titans were ranked seventh in the Northern California area in 1985.

Gary's senior year would prove to be an important one. He needed to impress the college scouts in order to earn an athletic scholarship. He was maturing into an all-around player and had gained the respect of his teammates. He enjoyed the role of being the team leader. "His work ethic was unbelievable," said Coach Noel. "He demanded it from his teammates, and wouldn't be afraid to get in their faces if he felt that they weren't giving it 100 percent out on the court."[10]

In another amazing game at the end of the season, Gary found himself facing several of the kids from his old neighborhood, who now attended rival Fremont High. Fremont was the best team in the league, and for Skyline to beat that team would be a huge accomplishment. The game was played hard from beginning to end. Then, with only seconds to go in the game, Gary drilled an off-balance jumper

FACT

Seven of Gary Payton's teammates at Skyline High School went on to earn Division I scholarships at major universities. Three played basketball, two played football, and two played baseball. (Of the three basketball players, Gary Payton plays with the SuperSonics, Greg Foster with the Jazz, and Kevin Stevenson played for the Warriors and the Blazers.)

to give Skyline the victory. It was a dramatic win for Skyline and a big confidence booster for Gary.

Skyline finished the season with an impressive 20–5 record, earning another Oakland Athletic League title. The team was also named as the 1986 Northern California Champions, and it would now play other California schools for the State Championship. The team then lost a one-point heartbreaker to De La Salle High School in a game in which Gary Payton fouled out. "The disappointment is what I remember most," said Payton years later. "I still think we were a lot better team than to lose in the first round."[11]

During Gary Payton's senior year, he averaged 20.6 points, 6.9 rebounds, and 10.5 assists per game, earned an All-American honorable mention, was the East Bay Player of the Year, and was named as an all-state and all-city selection. (In 1990 Skyline High School honored its greatest player ever, by retiring his No. 20 jersey into the rafters of the school's gymnasium.)

Gary Payton now had to decide where he wanted to go to college. His first choice was St. John's University in New York City. After the Titans had played in a basketball tournament in New York during his senior year, Gary became interested in attending the New York City university. He thought

Defense has always been the key to Gary Payton's success.

that the New York team would be perfect for his big-time style. Head coach Lou Carneseca was so impressed with the young point guard that he offered him a scholarship to attend St. John's. At the last minute, however, Carneseca decided to give the scholarship to another player, Marcus Broadnax. (Incidentally, Broadnax played only one season before leaving school.) Gary Payton was devastated.

Meanwhile, Gary's teammate Greg Foster received a lot of attention from the scouts because of his nearly seven-foot frame. He accepted a scholarship offer from the University of California at Los Angeles (UCLA). Gary was starting to wonder if he had what it took to make it at the next level. Many of the big-time recruiters had their doubts about his flamboyant personality, and they wondered if his attitude would be trouble for their team's chemistry.

Gary now had to do some soul searching. He had already received several offers to play Division I ball at some of the country's top schools, including Stanford, New Mexico State, North Carolina State, and Oregon State. His parents wanted him to get out of the big city. They liked the fact that the Oregon State coaches stressed academics and the importance of getting a college degree.

"Of all the schools that I visited," Gary said, "Oregon State was really the down-to-earth school.

Coach Anderson and the other people at Oregon State showed me what life would be like when I got there. They told my parents what they wanted out of me, what they thought they were going to get out of me, and what they thought I had the ability of doing."[12]

So, Gary packed up his 1967 Chevy (with license plates that read, "Mr. Icy") and headed north—up the Pacific Coast to Corvallis, Oregon. There, he would begin the next chapter of his career as a member of the Oregon State Beavers.

Chapter 3: How OSU Became "Payton's Place"

When Gary Payton arrived at Oregon State University (OSU), he was still bothered by the fact that St. John's had pulled his scholarship at the last second. He felt that he had a lot to prove.

The basketball season soon got under way, and Payton liked his new surroundings. He was eager to show the world just who Gary Payton was, and he wanted to jump right in. The transition from the high school game to the college game was like night and day. What separated the men from the boys was all the hard work on both ends of the court. Payton quickly learned that a good defensive play was often just as good, if not better, than a good offensive play. "Coach Noel at Skyline changed it up a little bit in my senior year to get me ready for college," he said. "Still, once I got here, I had to change from being offense-minded to defense-minded."[1]

As his first season progressed, there were ups and downs along the way. Payton found that he had to learn how to control his competitive personality. If a referee called a foul on him, he had to control his emotions and not explode. He soon became the guy that other teams loved to root against, but that just made him want to win that much more. "Gary is a team player and is a ball-handling catalyst," said assistant coach Jim Anderson of his new phenom. "He has all of the skills and basketball intellect to be considered a complete basketball player."[2]

The coaches worked with Payton to try to get him to settle down and control his temper. Big Al was not there any more to calm his son when he got frustrated, so Gary Payton had to learn for himself how to become a more relaxed player out on the court. "All that stuff, the talking and everything, came from playing playground ball in Oakland," Payton said.

> Back there, there used to be a lot of woofin', a lot of yap-yap. I just brought my playground game to college, and nobody else did. They didn't understand I didn't mean anything by it. It was just the way I grew up playing.[3]

Payton thrived at the collegiate level, posting scores in the double figures in 22 of 30 games, while tallying double figures in assists in six of those contests. In one game, he scored a career high of 20 points against Arizona, then grabbed 12 rebounds in a victory over Oregon. In addition to averaging nearly 13 points per game in his freshman year, he also averaged 7.6 assists per outing, en route to setting a new NCAA single-season freshman assists record. His 229 assists also broke the team record, held by one of the team's assistant coaches, Freddie Boyd, who had dished out 185 assists in 1972. (Payton, never shy about tooting his own horn, made sure to let his coach know that he had beaten his record every chance he got.) For his efforts, he was named both the PAC-10 (Pacific-10) Conference Rookie of the Year and Defensive Player of the Year. The Beavers advanced to the second round of the National Invitational Tournament (NIT), eventually losing to California University, 65–62.

As a sophomore, Payton was settling into his college routine. He was also becoming a sort of celebrity on campus. "Corvallis is a basketball town, and everything centers around the Beavers," said his roommate, Rodney Howard. "He's an idol to kids. Everybody looks up to him. He's like a Michael Jordan."[4]

Gary Payton's speed and quickness allowed him to run the fast break like no one before him at Oregon State.

Payton became so popular on campus that he had to rearrange his school schedule so he would only have classes on Tuesdays and Thursdays, partly because his presence caused such a commotion. Payton did not mind, though; he loved to sleep, and having three days off was just fine with him. On some of those days off, Payton participated in speaking engagements at local elementary schools to support antidrug programs. He even signed a statement that would allow him to be regularly tested for drugs.

Payton also took the time to get to know his fans, especially the young ones. After one game, as the team bus was waiting to leave, Payton stood in the cold and signed more than one hundred autographs. "I never want a break from the kids," he said.

FACT

On August 9, 1996, Payton not only was inducted into the Oregon State University Sports Hall of Fame, but his jersey, No. 20, was also retired high into the rafters of Gill Coliseum.

> All I think about is how I had role models, too, when I was little—like George Gervin. Now I'm thinking I've got to be a good role model because some little kid will want to grow up and be just like you and do the same things.[5]

In his second year at OSU, Payton continued to grow as an all-around player. He finished the season by scoring in double digits in nine consecutive games. He even poured in 30 points against OSU's in-state rivals from the University of Oregon. The Beavers finished the season in second place in the

PAC-10 conference, but the team lost to Louisville, 70–61, in the second round of the NIT. Payton, who was starting to get noticed on the national scene, received an honorable mention as an All-American selection and earned All-PAC-10 honors.

As Payton continued to gain exposure with the media, he found himself with a following wherever he went. Payton could always turn to one person when he wanted to get back to reality, though. His mom was at times her son's biggest critic and also his biggest fan. "She tells me the truth and tries to keep me honest," said Payton. "I'll be on the phone to my mother, and she'll say, 'Why don't you stop bragging; you're not that great.'"[6] Through it all, she kept Payton humble.

As Payton entered his junior season at OSU, he felt pressured to lead the team into the coveted NCAA Tournament, otherwise known as the Big Dance. One of the highlights of the year occurred in a game against St. Joseph's, in which Payton dished out his fourteenth assist of the night. With it, he surpassed George Tucker (525) as the OSU all-time assists leader. "I feel I can play with anybody in the country," Payton said. "I have a lot of confidence in my game. I don't think too many people can guard me one-on-one. I like passing the ball, too. When I start dishing off, it leads to me being able to score more."[7]

Flying through the air, Gary Payton, at times, seems to defy gravity.

Payton had become a complete player and team leader and was blossoming into a triple-threat performer. His shooting, passing, and defending skills were among the best in the conference. His hustle, great court sense, and unbelievable enthusiasm to win made him a crowd favorite at Gill Coliseum, OSU's home gym. "When I start playing well, the whole team plays well. It's just something that clicks," Payton said. "When I'm out there, I feel like I'm being a coach on the floor."[8]

Payton was awesome that season. He led the entire conference in scoring (21.8), assists (8.1), and steals (3.0) per game. Payton had finally guided OSU to the NCAA Tournament, where the team faced the University of Evansville. Despite Payton's 31 points and 10 assists, OSU was beaten in the first-round game, 94–90.

After that game, OSU head coach Ralph Miller, who had coached the Beavers for nineteen seasons, retired. His successor would be longtime assistant coach Jim Anderson, who had been an understudy at OSU for more than twenty-five years. For Payton, it was an emotional good-bye. "It was a great experience playing under Coach Miller because he taught me so much," Payton said.[9]

After the season was over, many scouts and people in the media were speculating that Payton might skip his senior year to join the NBA. However, Payton knew how much his mom wanted him to earn his college degree. That alone was enough for him to stay put and finish his senior year. Needless to say, the faithful fans of Corvallis were thrilled that they were going to have Payton for one more year.

Now that the pressure of entering the NBA draft was off, Payton relaxed and played ball. His senior campaign would prove to be one of the greatest single seasons ever registered by a college player. The NBA scouts came to all of his games and drooled over the possibility of having him lead their respective teams' offenses that next season. "A Gary Payton comes along once in ten years," said Marty Blake, the NBA's director of scouting.[10]

Payton's fame skyrocketed during his final year. "My first year in college I was OK," Payton said. "My second year I got better. My third year I was on the verge of being an All-American, and then my senior year—pow!—I'm Mr. Everything."[11]

The high point of the season happened on February 22, 1990, when the Beavers took on the Trojans of the University of Southern California. That night Payton broke OSU's career and single-game scoring records by putting in an unbelievable 58 points. In one of the most dramatic games in school

FACT

In Payton's four years at Oregon State University, he recorded 30 career double-double's (when a player scores double figures in two separate statistical categories in any one given game), and on November 26, 1988, he scored the school's only ever triple-double, with 20 points, 14 rebounds, and 11 assists against Portland.

Gary Payton was, without question, the big man on campus.

history, Payton almost single-handedly brought the Beavers back from a twenty-two-point deficit to beat the Trojans, 98–94, in an overtime thriller. Payton's 58 points not only set a Beaver all-time record, but also set the second highest single-game total in PAC-10 history. Through it all, Gary Payton exhibited his incredible talent and determined personality. "He's got that Ali way about him," said ESPN's Dick Vitale, referring to former boxing great Muhammad Ali.[12]

The Beavers finished the season strong. Payton led the team back to the NCAA Tournament in 1990, but were beaten in the first round by Ball State in a heartbreaker, 54–53. Payton finished the year averaging 25.7 points, 8.1 assists, 4.7 rebounds, and 3 steals per game. The end was finally here for Payton, but a very bright future lay ahead. With his degree in communications in hand, the new college grad now had the whole world in front of him. He had grown up, literally and figuratively. The once scrawny five-foot six-inch kid had grown and matured into a six-foot four-inch man.

Having started every game in his four seasons in Corvallis, the point guard simply rewrote the OSU record books. He averaged 18.1 points, 7.8 assists, and 4 rebounds per game, while shooting .485 from the floor, .700 from the line, and .333 from beyond the arc. He remains the school's all-time leader in total points (2,172), assists (938), and steals (321). He also finished in second place as the NCAA's all-time leader in steals and assists. Payton was named College Player of the Year by *Sports Illustrated*, PAC-10 Player of the Year by the conference coaches, and was a first-team pick on the NABC, UPI, and *The Sporting News* All-America teams. In addition, he was named to the PAC-10 All-Decade Team.

What was the next stop for the kid from "Oaktown" whose incredible defensive skills would earn him the nickname "the Glove"? The big time. The show. The NBA. The management of the Seattle SuperSonics saw Payton as the fiery leader who could guide their team into the future. So they selected him as the number-two overall pick in the 1990 NBA draft, behind the New Jersey Nets' number-one selection, Derrick Coleman, a power forward from Syracuse University. Gary Payton was an official lottery pick, and he was about to hit the lottery by signing a contract worth millions of dollars. Now the world would see what Oregon had seen over the past four years: Gary Payton was the real deal.

Chapter 4: "The Glove" Takes Seattle by Storm

The city of Seattle was eagerly anticipating the arrival of its highest draft pick in SuperSonics history. The pressure was on Gary Payton, since he had been named as the team's starting point guard on the first day that he walked into training camp. Most rookies would be eased into the lineup throughout the season, but with Payton's salary of $2.7 million per season, the team wanted to receive an instant dividend from its huge investment. Gary Payton (or "G. P." as he was known), not only had the eyes of the Seattle on him, but also those of the nation. Fans and media alike had put him under a microscope, watching his every move.

Payton brought with him an arsenal of

basketball weapons that included his tremendous defensive skills, unbelievable speed, and the ability to drive to the hoop through traffic. His tenacity to win, coupled with his skills, made him the rookie to watch in 1990. Seattle's fans had high hopes for Payton, who they felt would wonderfully complement their current team superstar, power forward Shawn Kemp.

As the season got under way, Payton quickly found that things did not come as easily for him in the NBA as they had at the collegiate level. The players were much bigger, faster, and stronger. In addition, his new coach, K. C. Jones, ran a drastically different offensive scheme than his coaches at Oregon State had. Payton felt uncomfortable in this new, slower system. He became tentative about shooting the ball because he knew that if he missed, he would get pulled from the game. While Payton wanted to run the ball up the court, Coach Jones wanted him to slow it down and exercise patience. Payton's confidence was growing weaker, and he did not know where to turn.

The Sonics finished the 1990–91 season at .500, with a record of 41–41. Payton started all 82 games for the team, averaging just 7.2 points per game on .450 field-goal shooting. He did, however, dish out 528 assists, for an average of 6.4 per outing, while

As one of the game's best defenders, Gary Payton can force his opponents to take poor shots.

snagging more than 2 steals per game, which ranked in the league's top twenty in both categories. Through it all, though, Payton was still voted to the NBA's All-Rookie Second Team. His numbers were acceptable, but he began to wonder whether he could be a star in the NBA. "The mental part was my fault because I let the coach get to me," said Payton.

> I questioned myself. I came home to Oakland that summer after my rookie year and I didn't work out. I thought I was through; one year in the league and that's that. I thought I would be bouncing around from team to team.[1]

In 1991, with a season under his belt, Payton returned to training camp with the hope of turning things around. His confidence was at an all-time low, and his jump shot was at about the same level. Despite a 7–3 start, Seattle finished the first half of the season at 20–20. The team was sputtering, and Payton became the subject of trade rumors. Something would have to give, and on January 23, 1991, it did. That was the day that Coach K. C. Jones was replaced by George Karl. Karl had learned to play the game under legendary coach Dean Smith at the University of North Carolina, and he had a lot in common with Payton. Karl, who was a player with the San Antonio Spurs in the mid-1970s, was also a fiery NBA point guard with an attitude.

FACT

Seattle's team name, the SuperSonics, was chosen because of the enormous Boeing airplane manufacturing plant located near the city. During the late 1960s, the company designed a Concorde-style airplane called the Supersonic Transport. Although the plane never made it off the ground, Washingtonians still decided to name their new basketball team the SuperSonics.

After leaving the Spurs, Karl had embarked on a coaching career that included stints with the Golden State Warriors, Cleveland Cavaliers, and most recently in the Continental Basketball Association (CBA). He was hired as the ninth skipper in team history. The key to Coach Karl's successful and winning coaching philosophy was the fact that he demanded that his players play defense. Karl took it upon himself to ensure that Payton became the team's leader, and he began working with him immediately. He knew that Payton had the potential to become an All-Star in the league, but he also knew that it was going to take a lot of hard work and determination on both of their parts to get there.

The two developed a special relationship. It was not always a rosy partnership, but they communicated and started to respect each other. One of the best decisions that Karl made during his first season was to hire assistant coach Tim Grgurich, who had been an assistant under Jerry Tarkanian at the University of Nevada at Las Vegas. Grgurich and Payton hit it off immediately and started to bond with each other. Grgurich took Payton under his wing and built up the young point guard's confidence by working with him on the fundamentals. "Coach 'Grg' was really the one who turned me around," Payton later said.[2]

The new chemistry was working. The Sonics had come full circle and began winning: Payton took to the head coach's new offense and started to enjoy the game of basketball again. Karl had also devised an innovative defensive strategy that was designed to disrupt opponents with relentless pressing, trapping, and double-teaming. It could not have been a more perfect fit for Payton.

Payton led the Sonics to a second-half rally, finishing the season with a 47–35 record, ranking the team fourth in the Pacific Division. Directing the offense and leading the defense, Payton guided the Sonics to a first-round playoff victory, three games to one, over the Golden State Warriors in front of his hometown fans in Oakland. The Sonics would go on to face the Utah Jazz in the NBA Western Conference Semifinals. In that series, the Sonics hung tough only to lose the series four games to one.

Playing nearly thirty-two minutes per game, Payton averaged 9.4 points on .451 shooting. He also led the team in steals (147) and assists (6.2) for the second straight year.

During the following off-season, Tim Grgurich invited Payton to his home in Utah to work out. It would prove to be great therapy for Payton, who was anxious to regain his old shooting touch. To boost Payton's confidence, the coach smartly took

Gary Payton and Shawn Kemp, a dynamic duo, were like thunder and lightning.

his pupil for a stroll around his property and reminded Payton what it was like when he was the big man on campus. "We actually walked for hours, and all we talked about was what I did at Oregon State," said Payton. "He didn't change my shot," said Payton.

> All he did was bring my confidence back. Before, I was thinking every time I shot the ball it was never going in, and now, each time I shoot I think the ball is going in. I don't care if I miss seven or eight shots in a row, I know eventually one is going to fall.[3]

Payton worked hard on improving his game during that off-season, and he was poised to have a breakthrough season in 1992–93. Karl was giving Payton the opportunity to run the offense, and it was working. Fresh from their playoff run, the Sonics were now a team to be reckoned with in the NBA's tough Western Conference.

The fragile relationship between Coach Karl and Payton, two rebel tough guys with big egos, was giving the Seattle media plenty to write about. Payton wanted still more control of the team, and more respect from his coach. Karl wanted Payton to become more of a team player. Karl was upset that Payton tried his patience, was often late for practices, and sometimes seemed not to care about

FACT

Payton scored two triple-doubles during the 1991–92 season against the Golden State Warriors (17 points, 12 assists, 11 rebounds) on December 21 and against the Utah Jazz (15 points, 13 assists, 10 rebounds) on March 31. The only other players to do so that year were Michael Jordan, Scottie Pippen, and David Robinson.

practicing. The two often got into arguments. Luckily, Coach Grgurich was there to serve as the mediator when things got too hot. Although rather unorthodox, this approach to communication worked for Karl and Payton. After airing out their grievances, they were able to set everything right again. As Payton explained,

> Coach Karl knows that he can't talk to me any way, and he won't let me talk to him just any way. We both have egos. He's got a big ego and I got a big ego, so he's not going to sit there and pick on me and single me out in front of individuals, because I'm not going to let that happen. Our solution is that, yeah, he can scream at me during practice or a game, but afterward, we go into his office and discuss what's going on. When everybody's not around, we can go in there and scream and holler and do what we have to do.[4]

At the end of my first season in Seattle, Gary and I met to talk about our future, said Karl.

> He and I had a list of three or four things. We wanted him to spend time working on his shot. We wanted him to participate in the summer mini-camps. We wanted him to get more aggressive offensively, to be more of a basketball player than a point guard. . . . I said,

Talking the talk, and walking the walk. That's Gary Payton.

'Gary, will you do these things?' He enthusiastically said he would do all those things. I said, 'If you do these things, I'll never ask to trade you. I'll give you the opportunity to become everything you want to become.'

Earlier in my career I would not have been smart enough to have had that meeting. I think I would have given up. I would have said, 'Get him out of here. Trade him.' Thank God I was never that stupid. I tell you, I'd hate to have to coach against Gary Payton, especially a Gary Payton who was motivated by the fact that we might have traded him.[5]

The 1992–93 season solidified Payton as a recognized point guard in the NBA. He was improving his shooting and was in sync with Shawn Kemp. From the thunderous dunks that Kemp provided to the lightning-quick passes that Payton dished to him, these two had become a real NBA dynamic duo. Payton had also been living up to his nickname, "the Glove," because on defense he was smothering and covering his opponents like a second skin. His darting moves and blink-of-an-eye dishes were freezing out defenders throughout the league, and his snarled upper lip was becoming his trademark.

Payton averaged 13.5 points, 4.9 assists, and 2.16 steals per contest that season. More important, he

One-on-one, Payton is one of the NBA's best.

had raised his shooting percentage from .400 to .494. It is safe to say that Payton's one thousand practice jump shots per day in the off-season were starting to pay big dividends. On November 27, he scored a season-high 31 points against the Dallas Mavericks; then, on March 13, he handed out 12 assists against the Miami Heat. Seattle had a 55–27 record that season, its second best in club history—ranking the team second in the Pacific Division.

Sonics players were hungry, and Payton was leading the charge. Seattle rolled through that regular season and right into the playoffs. The team's first opponent was Utah, who had knocked Seattle off only the year before. Payton worked the floor masterfully, setting up his teammates Shawn Kemp, Ricky Pierce, and Sam Perkins throughout the series. It came down to the wire, but Seattle prevailed, winning the series three games to two.

Next up was Hakeem Olajuwon and the Houston Rockets. In a back-and-forth contest, the Sonics beat the Rockets in a nail-biting seven-game series, prevailing 103–100 in an overtime thriller. Before Payton knew it, he had led his club all the way to the Western Conference Finals against Charles Barkley and the Phoenix Suns.

The Sonics played brilliantly throughout the series but lost four games to three. The team had come within only one game of meeting the mighty Chicago Bulls in the NBA Championships that year. Payton and company had gotten a taste of what it would be like to make it to the Finals. They knew they had to come back the next season and work even harder than ever before.

Chapter 5

Losing Two Heartbreakers

The SuperSonics had high expectations for the 1993–94 season. After making it all the way to the Western Conference Finals, the team felt that it was a legitimate contender to go all the way. The club had acquired forwards Detlef Schrempf and Kendall Gill in preseason trades, and it sprang out of the gate with a 20–2 record. Payton was excelling as well. In addition to his career-high 32 points against the Charlotte Hornets, he had also posted a career-high 8 steals against the Golden State Warriors. Payton and Coach Karl were also getting along better than ever, but Payton still detested going to practice. "He hates practice," said teammate Nate McMillan. "He hates warming up. He just wants to play. It's like as soon as a game starts, he says, 'Give me the ball.' He wants to play for something. Once something is on the line, he's there to play."[1]

Payton's disregard for workouts bothered Coach Karl, for whom practicing was essential. It all worked out, though, because Karl respected Payton's ability to get himself into game shape. "I can't imagine a better point guard for our style," Karl said. "There are some great point guards in this league, but there's not one I'd rather have playing for me than Gary."[2]

With an unstoppable offense that was led by a disruptive defense, Sonics players outscored their opponents by a league high of 9.2 points per game that year. They also won twenty-five games by at least twenty points, en route to a 63–19 record—a league best. They earned a number-one seed for the postseason, which also meant having the home-court advantage. Because Seattle had won thirty-seven of its forty-one regular-season home games, the team was optimistic about its chances. First up for Seattle in the best-of-five series was the eighth-seeded Denver Nuggets, a team that had finished the year with a record under .500.

Seattle routed the young Nuggets in Game 1, 106–82, in front of the fans at Seattle's Key Arena. The Sonics continued to roll in Game 2, winning

97–87. With a two-game lead, the series shifted back to Denver's McNichols Arena.

Game 3 would prove to be a pivotal one, as Denver won, 110–93. The momentum was starting to swing toward the upstart Colorado crew, and Payton could feel it. After the game, Payton was upset that his teammates were taking their opponents too lightly. That next night, things did not get much better for Seattle. The Sonics hung in there for the first three quarters, but the team could not score a field goal in the last one minute and twenty-two seconds of regulation time or the first four minutes and thirty seconds of overtime. Denver won the game, 94–85, to tie the series at two games apiece. Payton was furious.

It was back to Seattle for the fifth and final game of the series. The game was close through the first half, but Denver came out strong in the second half. With only a few minutes left, the defending Western Conference champs were down by seven points. Seattle fought back, though. With only seconds on the game clock, Payton, who was playing with an injured foot, put up a game-tying desperation shot. But out of nowhere came Nuggets center Dikembe Mutombo, who blocked the shot. Amazingly, Sonics guard Kendall Gill grabbed the rebound and put it in, to force an overtime period. Although the

Gary Payton makes the fine art of taking a defensive charging foul look so easy.

momentum was seemingly in Seattle's corner, the team came out in the extra session as flat as it had been all year. The Sonics proceeded to stun the basketball world by losing the game, 98–84. The crowd stood in shock after the game; they wanted to know how their team could let this happen. "I didn't come home [to Oakland] for about a month after the loss," Payton said. "I stayed in Seattle and thought about what happened. People around here are still talking about it. I know we'll hear about that for the whole . . . ['94–'95] season."[3]

Regardless of the loss, statistically, it was Payton's best season yet as a pro. He improved his scoring to 16.5 points per game, had 6 assists per game, and finished the year ranked seventh in the league in steals with 2.9 per contest. The fourth-year pro also achieved a career-best field goal accuracy of 50.4 percent. He was third among point guards. In addition to starting all 82 games, Payton also led the team in minutes played with 2,881. He also finished sixth in the league's MVP balloting, and was selected to the NBA's All-Defensive First Team and All-NBA Third Team. Both Payton and teammate Shawn Kemp represented the Sonics at the 1994 NBA All-Star Game. Payton also finished third in the balloting for the NBA's Most Improved Player Award. But, on the negative side, he shot an

FACT

On January 4, 1995, against the Cleveland Cavaliers, Payton set a team record for consecutive field goals made without a miss, by going 14 for 14. Only three other players in NBA history have gone 14 for 14 or better: Wilt "The Stilt" Chamberlain, Bailey Howell, and Billy McKinney.

embarrassingly low 59.5 percent from the free-throw line.

The Sonics players were anticipating the 1994–95 season as one of redemption. The teammates had all endured a rough off-season in which they had been unfairly labeled as *chokers*. Naturally, the players were eager to reestablish their team's reputation. Payton came out focused and determined to make it back to where the team was expected to be—the NBA Finals. As the team leader, the pressure was on Payton to guide the team back on track. Admittedly, he took a lot of the blame for the loss to Denver, and he vowed to take more responsibility the following season. He decided to relax, have some fun that year, and work hard to get back on top.

With his selections to both the All-Star Team and the All Defensive First Team, Payton had become a legitimate NBA superstar. He had also gained more confidence in himself and in his abilities. He was good, and occasionally he was not afraid to let his opponents know it. According to Coach Karl,

> When Gary is kind of asleep on the court, we almost try to get another player to antagonize him, because that's what stimulates him. He gets stimulated by other people thinking they're winning the battle with him. I've seen younger players in the NBA score on Gary and yap something to him. Nothing could make me

After scoring the winning hoop, Payton gets hugs and high fives from his Seattle teammates.

happier. I know we're okay then, because Payton will wake up and take on his challenger and usually just own him.⁴

"If I get emotional, my teammates are going to be emotional," Payton added. "If I'm playing hard, everybody is going to be playing hard and opponents are going to get riled and the crowd's going to start getting loud."⁵

The season was rolling along, and so were the Sonics. They were playing great basketball, and Payton was a man on a mission. He was even voted as the NBA Player of the Week on January 8, when he averaged 23.3 points, 4 rebounds, 8.7 assists, and 2.33 steals during the seven-day stretch.

At the midseason break the fans voted for Payton to play in his second consecutive All-Star Game. He thanked them by recording 6 points, 15 assists, 5 rebounds, and 3 steals to finish as the game's runner-up MVP, trailing behind guard Mitch Richmond of the Sacramento Kings. Then, in addition to establishing career highs with 33-point games on two different occasions, Payton also had a 32-point, 7-assist game against Portland.

With the playoffs once again in sight, bad news struck the Sonics. With only one week to go in the regular season, Payton suffered a broken finger on his left hand. He managed to play through the pain,

FACT

Ouch! In what was considered the worst defeat in Seattle sports history, the Sonics had gone from being the league's best team in the regular season, to becoming the first number-one seed ever to lose to a number-eight seed in the history of the NBA Playoffs, during the 1993–94 season.

The master of the head fake, Gary Payton can fake a defender out of his socks.

though, focused only on bringing an NBA Championship to the people of Washington State. The Sonics finished the season tied for the fifth-best record in the NBA at 57–25, good enough for only a fourth seed in the Western Conference Playoffs.

Seattle's first-round opponents would be the Los Angeles Lakers, who had given the Sonics trouble all season. The Sonics came out fighting, winning the first game convincingly in front of Seattle's faithful fans, 96–71. Then, in a twisted bit of déja vu, the Sonics lost three straight to experience their second consecutive first-round defeat. Simply put, the talent-laden squad just could not seem to achieve the right chemistry during the postseason.

Payton, still nursing a broken finger, shot a marginal 47.8 percent from the floor while managing a measly 21 assists and 5 steals in the four-game series. For Payton, it was devastating. He was not only sickened by the loss, but also did not want to become known as a player who could talk a good game but could not back it up in the playoffs. Payton knew that after their first-round upset losses in the last two seasons, in which point guards Robert Pack of the Nuggets and Nick Van Exel of the Lakers had outplayed him, he needed to play better, for the Sonics to win a championship. Statistically, it was another banner year. Payton averaged 20.6

points, 7.1 assists, and 2.5 steals per game. His .509 field-goal accuracy ranked fifth among NBA guards, and his free-throw shooting soared to a respectable .748. He was once again named to the All-Defensive First Team and moved up to the All-NBA Second Team. Payton also started and played in all 82 games, meaning that in his first five years in the league, he had missed only one game. Finally recognized as one of only a handful of elite point guards in the league, only a championship ring was eluding Gary Payton.

Chapter 6
Running With the Bulls

The weight of the world was on Gary Payton and his teammates as the 1995–96 season approached. Victimized by two unbelievable first-round upsets in consecutive seasons, the Sonics had to get their act together. "I have to step up," said Payton, who was again willing to assume more than his share of the blame for the team's postseason woes.[1]

The regular season soon got under way, and after back-to-back losses at both Indiana and Toronto, the Sonics had a record of 6–5. However, this record would mark the last time in the regular season that the Sonics would lose two straight games. From that point on, the team was officially on a roll. One of its biggest wins came in late November against the

Chicago Bulls. In that game, Payton stripped Michael Jordan of the ball in the final seconds to seal the victory. Amazingly, it would be one of only ten losses that Chicago would suffer all year long. Things were going well for the Sonics and also for Payton and Coach Karl, who were becoming good friends both on and off the court. "He's in the top 10 players in basketball right now," Karl said. "I don't think there's anybody who plays both ends of the court as well as he does."[2]

Payton added,

> I think George and I are just on the same page. He's like the father and I'm like the son. He knows he doesn't have to worry about the court. He can just worry about the bench. I make the decisions on the court. He just has to get us ready to play and I'm going to get it done for him. We're bonded together now. . . . He knew from the beginning I could be a great player and that's why he put so much confidence in me. He knew I could be the type of player I am now and he pushed me in that direction.[3]

The team was playing well, and it even posted a team-record fourteen-game winning streak in late February. On March 18, Payton registered his fourth triple-double (20 points, 10 rebounds, and 10 assists) against the L.A. Clippers. That next week, he dished out a career-high 17 assists against the Charlotte Hornets and then added a career-high of 38 points and 11 rebounds against Sacramento.

Once again Payton made his usual midseason appearance with the other superstars from around the NBA at the league's annual All-Star Game. Selected for the third consecutive time, Payton was now becoming a regular at the star-studded affair. Payton dazzled the crowd in San Antonio by scoring 18 points and adding 5 rebounds and 5 assists.

Payton was becoming a smarter player largely because of his penetrating and passing skills. Other teams were finding it difficult to defend the six-foot-four guard in the low post, as well as out on the three-point perimeter. If defenders left him open from long distance, he made them pay. One of his best defensive strategies was to overplay his man and force him to go in a different direction with the ball. This would allow him to then come across from the other side and pick the ball off for a steal. Payton knew that when opposing teams had to guard him with their shooting guards, rather than their smaller, quicker point guards, it was a mismatch that Payton was going to capitalize on every time.

The Sonics rolled through the season and quietly posted a 64–18 record—good enough to earn the team its tenth-best season in NBA history. However,

Gary Payton's defense often led to turnovers, which, in turn, led to fast breaks in the transition for the Sonics.

the people of Seattle were not about to get excited about a great regular season. Given their team's track record over the past two seasons in the playoffs, the players made it clear they were not going to be satisfied with anything less than a trip to the NBA Finals.

Sacramento, yet another eighth-seeded team, was first up for the Sonics in the opening round of the playoffs. The pressure was immense for the Sonics; the eyes of the nation were waiting to see if they could get back on the winning track. Seattle players also learned that they were going to be without their All-Star forward Shawn Kemp for Game 1. Kemp was given a one-game suspension for a fight that took place during the team's regular-season finale. It was now up to Payton, who was playing with a bad cold, to carry the load for Seattle. Payton, as usual, responded in a big way, recording 29 points, 9 assists, 6 rebounds, and 4 steals in a 97–85 win. "Gary had big shoulders for us," said Coach Karl after the game. "We just rode him all night long."[4]

Game 2 was a struggle for Seattle. Still feeling ill, Payton could only contribute 10 points and 7 assists. Sacramento won the game, 90–81, to tie the best-of-five series. Fans were starting to get nervous, but the Sonics players remained calm. With their backs against the wall, they came out swinging in Game 3, which had now moved to Sacramento. The Sonics rallied from a ten-point second-half deficit to beat the Kings, 96–89. Full of confidence, the Sonics buried the Kings in Game 4, 101–87, to win the series.

Seattle had beaten the opening-round loss omen that had plagued them for the previous two seasons. The team now faced the two-time defending champion, the Houston Rockets, in round two. Payton had averaged nearly 29 points per game against the Rockets that year. He was encouraged by the fact that Seattle had beaten the Rockets in the last nine straight contests. Following Payton's lead, the Sonics came out and convincingly took Game 1, 108–75. In that game, Payton hit four early three-pointers and finished with 28 points and 7 assists. His thirteen tries from behind the three-point line in the first two quarters set an NBA Playoffs record for the most three-point attempts in a half.

The Sonics took Game 2, 105–101, as Payton continued to dominate with 18 points, 5 rebounds, and 5 assists. Payton scored 28 points in Game 3 and nailed 2 free throws with ten seconds left to give the Sonics a 115–112 win. In Game 4, Payton poured in 24 points and added 11 assists in a 114–107 overtime victory. Led by Payton's stifling defense, the Sonics

Giving the referee an earful, Gary Payton pleads his case.

shut down All-Star center Hakeem Olajuwon and swept the defending champs four games to none.

The Sonics players were on cruise control and knew that they were in command of their own destiny. The team's next stop was the Western Conference Finals, this time against the Utah Jazz. Playing against All-Stars Karl Malone and John Stockton was going to be a tough task, but Payton and company were up for it. "Talking won't win this series," said Payton. "Both teams are just going to come and lay their cards on the table. All that's definite is that the winner will have to beat a pair of aces."[5]

In Game 1, Payton held the crafty veteran John Stockton to a mere 4 points and 7 assists, preventing him from executing his specialty: the penetration and pass. Meanwhile, Payton posted 21 points, 7 assists, 4 rebounds, and 3 steals to lead the Sonics past the Jazz, 102–72. The series was back and forth, with Seattle taking Game 2. Utah came back, and took Game 3. Seattle rallied to take Game 4, only to lose Games 5 and 6. It was now down to Game 7 for the title. Payton rose to the occasion with 21 points, 6 rebounds, and 5 assists in a 90–86 victory. Seattle had done it; for the first time since their 1979 Western Conference Championship series against Washington, the Sonics were going to the NBA

FACT

On March 15, 1996, something unusual happened to the Sonics while playing against the Dallas Mavericks. Due to an NBA-levied suspension, Payton's consecutive-games-played streak came to an end at 354. Up to that point, "Mr. Durable" had missed only one game in six seasons, and that was due to an illness.

Finals. "I told our guys we looked like [baby] robins in the nest, mouths open, waiting for the ball to fall in," said Jazz coach Jerry Sloan after the game. "On defense, as quick as the Sonics are on film, they look like they have six defenders out there. Today, it looked like they had 10 guys."[6]

Seattle's opponent in the NBA Finals was none other than the Chicago Bulls, against whom Seattle had split two games during the regular season. Game 1 of the Finals, which took place in Chicago, got off to a rocky start for Payton. The Bulls were double-teaming him whenever he had the ball and disrupting his game plan. Ron Harper, who was a full two inches taller than Payton, was hounding him the entire game. Payton missed his first six attempts and did not get into the scoring column until the second quarter. Defensively, Coach Karl did not want Payton to get fatigued, or to get into foul trouble, so he kept him away from "Air" Jordan. The plan was futile, as Chicago won big, 107–90. Shawn Kemp scored 32 points, while Payton finished with only 10 points and 6 assists in the defeat.

In Game 2, the Bulls' swarming defense was again causing problems for the Sonics. Chicago's strategy was to put tight coverage on Payton and force him to play tentatively. Payton tried to get back into the game, at times even firing verbal jabs at his "Airness," Michael Jordan. The Bulls won again, this time by a score of 92–88. Gary Payton could manage only 13 points and 3 assists in the loss.

Game 3 moved back to Seattle's Key Arena, where more than seventeen thousand screaming fans welcomed home their Sonics. Michael Jordan came out strong, scoring 27 first-half points and 36 overall, giving the Bulls the victory. Despite Payton's 19 points and 9 assists, the Sonics, down three games to none, again found themselves on the brink of elimination.

The Sonics had nothing to lose in Game 4, and came out to play for team pride. Chicago, however, with a record of 14–1 in the playoffs at that point, was eager to finish off the Sonics. Payton and Kemp came out smoking and hooked up on an alley-oop slam that rocked the rim. It was a statement to the Bulls: The team could not come onto the Sonics home court and push its players around. Shortly thereafter, Payton buried a three-pointer that brought the fans to their feet. Payton, who was finally playing relaxed, was in the zone once again. His three-pointer launched a 13–2 run for the Sonics, as the team took a 25–21 lead at the end of the first quarter.

Payton shows his frustration as he throws his hands up in the air.

Seattle then came out and scored the first eleven points of the second quarter. Jordan, who was struggling all night, was uncharacteristically called for an offensive foul, which then turned into a technical foul. The incident gave the Sonics even more momentum, and the team took a 53–32 lead into halftime. Chicago's meager 11 points had tied the record for the fewest points ever scored in a quarter of an NBA Finals contest. Seattle rolled in the second half and put the Bulls' victory party on ice, at least for the time being. In addition to Shawn Kemp's 25 points, Payton added 21 points, 11 assists, and 2 steals in the 107–86 victory. It was only the second time during the season that the Bulls had lost a game by more than ten points.

Seattle continued to rock and roll, beating the Bulls again in Game 5, 89–78. Payton's game-high of 23 points led the way for the Sonics, and Payton's stifling defense shut down Jordan and Pippen. Full of confidence, Seattle headed back to Chicago for the pivotal Game 6.

Back in Chicago, the Bulls ended the Sonics' title hopes by winning Game 6, 87–75. Once again, the Championship ring had eluded Payton and his teammates. He did, however, earn Jordan's respect. The two had been compared with each other all series long, and many people believe that Payton will be the one in the league to carry the torch now that Michael Jordan has decided to hang up his sneakers. Even though the Bulls prevailed, Payton had proven that he could lead his team to the Finals. "I think the thing that Michael Jordan and Gary Payton have in common is a competitive heart," said Coach Karl. "Michael might have more skills, have more talent, and have more ability to do this and do that, but Gary Payton can match Michael Jordan as a competitor, and that's saying a heck of a lot."[7]

Payton started all twenty-one playoff games, averaging 20.7 points, 5.1 rebounds, and team-highs of 6.8 assists and 1.76 steals in 43.4 minutes per game. For the season, Payton averaged 19.3 points, 7.5 assists, and 2.85 steals. Leading the league in steals, he was named as the NBA Defensive Player of the Year. He was also named to his third straight All-Defensive First Team, and was finally named to the All-NBA First Team. Payton was rewarded for his solid play during the off-season, when he was selected to become a member of the Dream Team that won a gold medal for the United States at the 1996 Olympics in Atlanta.

Chapter 7

The Future Is Bright

After bringing home the gold from the Atlanta Olympics in 1996, Payton, now a free agent, had the option to either remain with the Sonics or entertain offers from other NBA teams that wanted him to come play for them. Several teams wanted him to jump ship, but Payton decided to stay in Seattle, and he was rewarded with a seven-year, $89.5-million contract.

Committed to the city of Seattle, Gary Payton wanted to give something back to the community that had been so good to him. In 1996 he established the Gary Payton Foundation to help underprivileged young people. The foundation provides opportunities in education, recreation, and overall wellness to at-risk young people who are deprived of basic options in life. Among the events that the foundation sponsors is the Gary Payton All-Star Classic charity basketball game, which benefits the Big Brothers of King County. The Gary Payton Foundation Endowment Scholarship provides financial assistance to a student from Washington who is attending a United Negro College Fund university and otherwise would not be able to attend college. "I have always held a spot in my heart for children, especially children in need," Payton said. "I quickly recognized my NBA career could open doors that would create opportunities for kids to achieve their dreams. My foundation allows me to help them on a full-time basis."[1]

Payton's Glove Club summer basketball camp is for inner-city young people who want to improve their skills both on and off the court. In addition, Payton hosts holiday parties for sick children at Children's Hospital; talks to Seattle Public School District kids about the importance of reading; and purchases and distributes Sonics game tickets for underprivileged young people and their families. To date, the Gary Payton Foundation has raised more than half a million dollars for charities. "Ever since I was a little boy in Oakland, it has been my dream to make it in the NBA," said Payton.

> Fortunately, I was blessed with many opportunities in life to achieve my dream. I only hope that the Gary Payton Foundation will provide other children with opportunities to achieve their dreams in life.[2]

Determined to bring a championship to the Seattle fans, Payton focused his energy on the upcoming 1996–97 season. The Sonics had high expectations that year, and anything short of a return trip to the NBA Finals would be regarded as a subpar season. Payton had another good year, recording two triple-doubles and also scoring a season high of 32 points against Orlando on March 4. Once again Payton was voted to the All-Star Team, in which he tallied 17 points and handed out a team-high 10 assists in twenty-eight minutes of play.

Seattle won its final three games to finish the regular season with a 57–25 record, good enough for its third Pacific Division crown in four years. The Sonics also became the first club ever to lead the league in steals for five straight seasons (11.02 per game).

Gary Payton was on cruise control, and the people of Seattle were eager to let him lead them

Payton tries to give back to the community. He hosts holiday parties for sick children at Children's Hospital and talks to Seattle Public School District kids about the importance of reading, among other things.

The Future Is Bright

back to the NBA Finals. "Five years ago Gary had a lot of people who did not believe in him, from his teammates to many fans in Seattle," said Coach Karl. "A number of NBA people did not think he was much of a player. Right now every team would love to have him. Right now I think he is the best point guard in the NBA."[3]

The Sonics went on to face Phoenix in the playoffs. After trailing two games to one, the team rallied to beat the Suns in five. In the final game of the series, the Sonics blew a twenty-two-point lead before regrouping to earn a 116–92 victory. Next up were the Houston Rockets and Charles Barkley.

Again, Seattle fell behind three games to one, only to rally and beat Houston in Game 5. Back in Seattle for Game 6, Payton had 19 points, 13 assists, and 5 steals to get his club a twenty-two-point lead. Houston came back, though, narrowing the margin to two points with only thirty seconds to go. Then, in the final seconds, Payton's spinning left-handed hook shot locked up a 99–96 victory.

In the pivotal Game 7, the Sonics rallied from a fourteen-point, fourth-quarter deficit, closing within two points in the final minute. Payton led the charge, playing with the same intensity that had earned his squad a trip to the Finals the year before. At the end, Houston, led by Matt Maloney's

FACT

In July 1997, Payton and his longtime sweetheart, Monique (a former basketball star at Oakland's Skyline High School, who also played basketball at the junior college level), were married. Together they have two children, Gary, Jr., and Raquel, and they live in a suburb of Oakland.

three-point assault, played tougher and held on for the 96–91 win. For Payton, it was yet another devastating end to a great season.

For the year, Payton would average 21.9 points per game, ranking tenth in the NBA in scoring. He also averaged 7.1 assists per game, was third in the league in steals with 2.4 per outing, and had a career-high 119 three-pointers. In addition to being named to the All-Defensive First Team and the All-NBA Second Team, Payton finished second only to Atlanta's Dikembe Mutombo in the balloting for the league's Defensive Player of the Year Award.

The Sonics came into training camp for the 1997–98 season without a familiar face in the line-up. During the off-season the team was involved in a three-way trade with both Milwaukee and Cleveland that sent All-Star power forward Shawn Kemp to the Cleveland Cavaliers and brought Vin Baker to Seattle. After losing in the playoffs, Sonics management thought that a shakeup would do the team some good. Baker, himself a three-time All-Star power forward, would fit in nicely in Seattle.

The Sonics got off to another great start that season. Teams learned that the best way to stop Payton was to come right at him. Opposing teams used their biggest guards, often double- or triple-teaming him when he posted up to the basket. Teams were

Talk about hang time, Gary Payton can flat out fly.

being forced to change their game plans to defend Gary Payton. "I'm taking what they give me," said Payton. "That's all. If they want to double- and triple-team me, I'm going to give the ball to the open people."[4]

As the Sonics and Lakers battled for first place in the Western Conference, Payton was quietly among the league's leaders in points, assists, and steals. He was again voted to start for the Western Conference in the All-Star Game. In his fifth straight All-Star appearance, he handed out a game-high 13 assists. Payton had also received the fifth most All-Star votes in the league that year, solidifying him as a bona fide superstar with the fans.

It was another stellar year for both Payton and the Sonics. Payton scored a season high of 31 points against Vancouver on November 11 and registered at least 14 assists in eight different games. He had at least 5 steals in seven games, dished out more than 10 assists in twenty-one games, and led the team in scoring thirty-one times. On March 18, 1998, Payton scored the ten thousandth point of his career against the Minnesota Timberwolves. Even though the league's best man-on-man defender was making a strong statement that he was a legitimate MVP candidate, he remained focused. "I'm not thinking about [the MVP]," he said. "I'm thinking about winning a championship."⁵

Having once again started all eighty-two games, Payton led the Sonics in assists, steals, and minutes played. The team captain finished sixth in the league with 8.3 assists per game. He was among the NBA's top twenty in scoring, with 19.2 points per game, and was named to the All-NBA and Defensive All-NBA First Teams. When it was all said and done, Seattle was once again sitting alone atop the Pacific Division with an impressive 61–21 record. The Sonics had become only the third team ever to win fifty-five or more games in six consecutive seasons. The new tandem of Payton and Baker was making a lot of noise that year at Key Arena. "Gary is a great passer even more so than other great point guards," said Vin Baker, "because he can break down a defense and then spot open people."⁶

That year's first-round playoff opponent would be the Minnesota Timberwolves, a team led by power forward Kevin Garnett and point guard Stephon Marbury. The T-Wolves took the lead in the series two games to one. Then Payton took things into his own hands, averaging nearly 27 points per game to lead Seattle to a three-games-to-two victory.

In the next round, the Sonics faced the Lakers. Seven-footer Shaquille O'Neal and high school

FACT

In 1998 Payton starred in his first national television commercial for the Nike shoe company. The campaign, called "the Fun Police," starred Payton as a detective who wears a yellow trenchcoat and busts young ball-hogging basketball players who cause the game to be boring.

phenom Kobe Bryant led the Lakers. Los Angeles had also finished the regular season with a 61–21 record and matched up well with Seattle. In the end, though, the Lakers overwhelmed the Sonics. Despite Payton's 22 points and 8.4 assists per game, Los Angeles won the series in five games. Once again, it was an early exit from the playoffs for Payton.

Big changes came about during that off-season. On June 17 the team announced that former Phoenix Suns head coach Paul Westphal and his high-scoring offensive coaching style would take over the head coaching reins from George Karl. (Karl went on to become the coach and general manager of the Milwaukee Bucks.) Other changes included Nate McMillan's becoming an assistant coach and the release of veteran forwards Dale Ellis and Sam Perkins. Also at the beginning of the 1998–99 season, the NBA declared a lockout. Because of the escalating salaries in the league, team owners felt they needed to reassess players' contracts. Unfortunately for the fans, the season was postponed until February 1999. However, a new labor agreement was established between the NBA owners and its players, ensuring that the league would be in good shape for the upcoming millennium.

Even though Timberwolves forward Kevin Garnett had a great series, the Sonics held tough and won the first round playoff series in 1997.

With a new labor agreement finally reached, the NBA was able to salvage a shortened 50-game season in 1998–99. The Sonics, however, ended the season with a disappointing 25–25 record and for the first time since 1990, did not make the playoffs. The team, which went 18–7 at home, and 7–18 on the road, finished fifth in the Pacific Division behind Portland, Los Angeles, Phoenix, and Sacramento respectively. Payton got the Sonics out of the gates with a flurry though, as he was named as the NBA's Player of the Week for the week ending February 14, after averaging an impressive 26.4 points per game, 9 assists per game, 5.8 rebounds, and 2 steals to lead the club to a 5–0 start.

Another highlight that season came on March 1, when Payton tallied a triple-double, with 28 points, a game-high 12 assists and 10 rebounds, and added 3 steals in a 105–102 win over the Sacramento Kings. Payton also logged some memorable stats that season. On February 10, he notched his fifteen hundredth career steal, posting a game-high 24 points, 11 assists, 7 rebounds, and 3 steals, in an 89–82 win over the Golden State Warriors. Then, later that week on February 16, he swiped his twenty-five hundredth career rebound, recording game-highs of 17 points, 11 rebounds, and 8 assists, in a 71–56 victory over the Utah Jazz. Finally, on

March 29, Payton sank his five hundredth career three-pointer, registering a game-high 20 points, 7 assists, and 4 rebounds, in a 109–101 win over the Dallas Mavericks.

Despite the team's marginal record, all in all it was a good year for Payton, who finished sixth in league scoring with 21.7 points per game, fourth in the league with 8.7 assists per game, and seventh in the league with 2.18 steals per game. In addition, Payton recorded 19 double-doubles and added 83 three-pointers for the Sonics. For his efforts, Payton was named to the 1998–99 NBA All-Defensive First Team and to the 1998–99 All-NBA Second Team.

During the off-season, the Sonics gave Payton a firm commitment that they were going to improve their squad, and get him a better supporting cast. Resigning all-star forward Vin Baker, who was hurt for much of the 1998–99 season, was the first big step to getting the team back into contention. While the club acquired all-star power forward Horace Grant from Orlando, and guards Vernon Maxwell and Brent Barry from Sacramento and Chicago respectively, it also said good-bye to veterans Detlef Schrempf and Hersey Hawkins. The team also fortified its frontcourt by reuniting Payton with his old Skyline High School teammate, center Greg Foster, who had been with the Utah Jazz.

Seattle is one of the premier clubs in the NBA, and Gary Payton, who will be a sure bet to be a league MVP candidate, is continuing to lead the way. His Nike shoe commercials make him the company's top NBA pitchman in the post-Jordan era. Who knows, with Michael Jordan out of basketball now, maybe Payton will finally become the league's MVP. "I really don't think about that stuff," said Payton.

> I have four other guys I start with and seven more on the bench, and if I won the award, I would have to give it to those guys. They are the ones that make it happen. I mean I can't just go out there and play by myself. All I can do is try to make the people around me play better.[7]

Gary Payton will undoubtedly go down in the annals of basketball history as one of the great ones. An unbelievable offensive and defensive threat, he is that rare talent who can score *and* guard his counterparts like a glove. He has the whole package: quickness, toughness, attitude, and intensity. His piercing glare, snarled upper lip, relentless pressure, and keen anticipation intimidate his opponents, creating offensive opportunities for his team. Payton is without question one of the best defenders in the NBA. The future is definitely looking bright for

Payton and the Sonics. Most important, though, Payton is a role model for young people everywhere, proving firsthand that hard work, determination, and discipline, combined with pure raw talent, can be a recipe for success in life. "When my career is over in the NBA, I want to look back with no regrets and be proud of what I was able to accomplish not only on the court, but off the court as well," said Payton.[8] Gary Payton is well on his way to achieving that goal.

Chapter Notes

Chapter 1.   Going for Gold

1. "Dream Teamer Payton in Right Place at Right Time," *San Francisco Examiner*, July 20, 1996, p. 1.

2. Ibid.

3. David DuPree, "Evolution of an All-Star," May 1996, <http://www.NBA.com/playoffs98/00671512> (November 5, 1998).

4. Howard Blatt, *Dream Team III: Quest for the Gold* (New York: Simon & Schuster, Inc., 1996), p. 155.

5. "Dream Team Steps Up, Routs China 133–70," *USA Today*, July 27, 1996, p. C3.

Chapter 2.   Hoop Dreams From Oakland

1. "Personality Change Profound," *The Statesman Journal* (Oregon), December 24, 1989, p. E5.

2. Dan Dieffenbach, "Pressure Point," *Sport*, January 1995, p. 94.

3. "In My House," *Esquire*, December 1997, p. 108.

4. Kirkpatrick, pp. 31–34.

5. Jake Curtis, "A Cool Man at the Point," *The Chronicle* (Oregon), January 5, 1995, p. 42.

6. Kirkpatrick, pp. 31–34.

7. Author interview with Fred Noel, November 2, 1998.

8. Ibid.

9. Kirkpatrick, pp. 31–34.

10. Author interview with Fred Noel.

11. "Gary Payton," *Cal High School Sports Alumni Spotlight*, January 16, 1990.

12. Ken Wheeler, "Payton's Hurt Forgotten in Success With OSU," *The Oregonian*, December 24, 1989, p. E1.

Chapter 3.   How OSU Became Payton's Place

1. "Gary Payton," *Cal High School Sports Alumni Spotlight*, January 16, 1990.

2. Oregon State University Men's Basketball Media Guide (Eugene, Oregon 1990), p. 1.

3. Phil Taylor, "Payton Lets His Play Do His Talking Now," *The National*, February 28, 1990, p. 15.

4. "Personality Change Profound," *The Statesman Journal* (Oregon), December 24, 1989, p. E5.

5. Tim Kelly, "Payton Plays Model Role," *The Gazette Times* (Oregon), February 24, 1990, p. B1.

6. "Personality Change Profound," p. E5.

7. "Winning Games, If Not Attention," *The New York Times*, December 12, 1989, p. D3.

8. Ibid.

9. "Personality Change Profound," p. E5.

10. Shannon Fears, "Sitting on Top of His World," *The Register Guard* (Oregon), February 2, 1990, pp. C1–C2.

11. Dan Dieffenbach, "Pressure Point," *Sport*, January 1995, p. 94.

12. "Personality Change Profound," p. E4.

Chapter 4. The Glove Takes Seattle by Storm

1. Dan Dieffenbach, "Pressure Point," *Sport*, January 1995, p. 94.

2. Ibid.

3. Ibid.

4. Ibid.

5. George Karl and Don Yeager, *The Game's the Best* (New York: St. Martin's, 1997), pp. 183–196.

Chapter 5. Losing Two Heartbreakers

1. "Payton Backs Up All His On-the-Court Talk," <http://nando.net> (April 28, 1996).

2. Phil Taylor, "Talk Show," *Sports Illustrated*, May 27, 1996, pp. 34–38.

3. Dan Dieffenbach, "Pressure Point," *Sport*, January 1995, p. 94.

4. George Karl and Don Yeager, *The Game's the Best* (New York: St. Martin's, 1997), pp. 183–196.

5. Terry Frei, "OSU's Payton Keeps Up the Pressure," *The Oregonian*, December 4, 1989, p. C3.

Chapter 6. Running With the Bulls

1. "Spotlight: Gary Payton," *Sports Illustrated for Kids*, November 1996, p. 56.

2. "Payton Backs Up All His On-the-Court Talk," <http://nando.net> (April 28, 1996).

3. David DuPree, "Evolution of an All-Star," November 5, 1998, <http://www.NBA.com/playoffs98/00671512.html> (November 18, 1998).

4. Phil Taylor, "Talk Show," *Sports Illustrated*, May 27, 1996, p. 38.

5. Phil Taylor, "For Payton, the Torch Is Waiting," *Sports Illustrated*, May 27, 1996, p. 47.

6. Art Thiel, "To the Point," *The Sporting News*, May 27, 1996, p. 49.

7. David DuPree, "A Winning Bond, Karl and Payton Have Special Relationship," *USA Today*, April 6, 1998, p. C1.

Chapter 7. The Future Is Bright

1. "The Payton Report," © 1998, <http://www.gpfoundation.org> (April 27, 1998).

2. Ibid.

3. George Karl with Don Yeager, *The Game's the Best* (New York: St. Martin's Press, 1997), pp. 183–196.

4. Nunyo Demasio, "Payton Makes Silent Point," *Seattle Times*, December 10, 1997, <http://www.seattletimes.com/extra/browse/html97> (November 18, 1998).

5. Sam Smith, "Payton Becomes MVP (More Valuable Person)," *Chicago Tribune*, January 13, 1998, p. 4.

6. Demasio, <http://www.seattletimes.com/extra/browse/html97>.

7. "Up Close," ESPN television network interview, February 19, 1999.

8. "Olympic Gold Medalist and Sonic Point Guard Gary Payton Establishes Foundation to Benefit Underprivileged Children," © 1998, <http://www.gpfoundation.org> (April 27, 1998).

Career Statistics

Year	Team	G	MPG	FG%	FT%	REB	AST	STL	BLK	PTS	AVG
1990–91	Sonics	82	27.4	.450	.711	243	528	165	15	588	7.2
1991–92	Sonics	81	31.5	.451	.669	295	506	147	21	764	9.4
1992–93	Sonics	82	31.1	.494	.770	281	399	177	21	1,110	13.5
1993–94	Sonics	82	35.1	.504	.595	269	494	188	19	1,349	16.5
1994–95	Sonics	82	36.8	.509	.716	281	583	204	13	1,689	20.6
1995–96	Sonics	81	39.0	.484	.748	339	608	231	19	1,563	19.3
1996–97	Sonics	82	39.2	.476	.715	378	583	197	19	1,785	21.8
1997–98	Sonics	82	38.4	.453	.744	376	679	185	18	1,571	19.2
1998–99	Sonics	50	40.2	.434	.721	244	336	109	12	1,084	21.7
Totals		704	34.8	.477	.712	2,706	4,716	1,603	157	11,503	16.3

G-Games
MPG-Minutes per Game
FG%-Field Goal Percentage
FT%-Free Throw Percentage
REB-Rebounds
AST-Assists
STL-Steals
BLK-Blocks
PTS-Points
AVG-Average

Where to Write Gary Payton

Mr. Gary Payton
c/o Seattle SuperSonics
190 Queen Anne. N. #200
Seattle, WA 98109

On the Internet at:
http://www.nba.com/Sonics
http://www.gpfoundation.org

Index

A
Ali, Muhammad, 16
Anderson, Jim, 38

B
Baker, Vin, 86, 89, 93
Barkley, Charles, 8, 14, 55
Barry, Brent, 92
Bird, Larry, 9
Bryant, Kobe, 90

C
Carneseca, Lou, 28
Chamberlain, Wilt, 61
Coleman, Derrick, 42

D
Divac, Vlade, 14
Dream Team, 7–10, 12–14, 16–17, 80–81

E
Ellis, Dale, 90

F
Foster, Greg, 24, 25, 28, 93
Fremont High School, 25

G
Garnett, Kevin, 89, 91
Gary Payton Foundation, 81–82
Gervin, George, 21, 35
Gill, Kendall, 56, 59

Grant, Horace, 93
Grgurich, Tim, 47–51

H
Harper, Ron, 76
Hawkins, Hersey, 93

J
Jefferson Elementary School, 21
Johnson, Magic, 9
Jones, K.C., 44, 46
Jordan, Michael, 9, 70, 77, 79, 80, 94

K
Karl, George, 46, 62, 70, 80, 90
Kemp, Shawn, 49, 53, 61, 72, 76, 86

M
Malone, Karl, 14, 75
Maloney, Matt, 85
Marbury, Stephon, 89
Maxwell, Vernon, 92
McMillan, Nate, 57, 90
Miller, Ralph, 38
Miller, Reggie, 14, 17
Mutumbo, Dikembe, 59, 86

N
Nike, 89
Noel, Fred, 22, 24

O

O'Neal, Shaquille, 12, 13, 89
Oakland, California, 19, 20, 21, 22, 23, 24, 25, 26
Oakland Athletic League, 22–23
Oakland Neighborhood Basketball League, 20
Olajuwon, Hakeem, 14, 55, 75
Oregon State University, Corvallis, 31, 32, 33, 35, 36, 38, 39, 41, 42

P

Pack, Robert, 66
Payton Family, 17
Payton's Glove Club, 82
Payton, Al, 19–29
Payton, Monique, 85
Perkins, Sam, 55, 90
Pierce, Ricky, 55
Pippen, Scottie, 14, 79

S

Schmidt, Oscar, 13
Schrempf, Detlef, 56, 93
Skyline High School, 21, 22, 25, 26, 85
Sloan, Jerry, 76
Smith, Dean, 46
Stockton, John, 8, 16, 75

V

Van Exel, Nick, 66

W

Westphal, Paul, 90

Eastlake Public Library
36706 Lake Shore Blvd.
Eastlake, OH 44095
APR 2 0 2000